In memory of Marvin, a loving grandfather and magician

DIAL BOOKS FOR YOUNG READERS
Penguin Young Readers Group
An imprint of Penguin Random House LLC
375 Hudson Street
New York, NY 10014

Text copyright © 2017 by Jacky Davis
Illustrations copyright © 2017 by David Soman

Manufactured in China on acid-free paper
ISBN 9780803740327
10 9 8 7 6 5 4 3 2 1

Designed by Jasmin Rubero
Text set in Old Claude

The art was created in ink and watercolor.

Ladybug Girl's Day Out with Grandpa

by David Soman and Jacky Davis

Dial Books for Young Readers

"I can't wait to see dinosaurs, birds, elephants, emeralds, bears, lions, planets, and whales," Lulu tells her grandpa.
"Oh!" she adds. "And stingrays too!"

Grandpa is taking her to the natural history museum.
"I want to learn *everything* about *everything*!" Lulu says.

"There is a lot to see here," Grandpa tells her.

"We won't be able to learn about *everything* in one day."

"I can do it," Lulu insists. "I'm Ladybug Girl!"

Inside, there is a mighty mama dinosaur protecting her baby.

It makes Lulu's wings flutter with excitement.

"What do you want to see next?" Grandpa asks Lulu.

"More dinosaurs!" she declares.

But as they walk to the elevators, Lulu calls,
"Wait, Grandpa! Look over here—elephants!
Let's learn about the elephants!"
Then something else catches her eye. "What is that, Grandpa?"

Before he can tell her that it's a Cape buffalo, Lulu is already turning toward . . .

The bears!

"Doesn't that one look like my teddy bear Blueberry, Grandpa? Can we learn about bears now?"

"We can, but hold on—we can't learn about dinosaurs *and* Cape buffalo *and* bears all at the same time."

"Okay, dinosaurs first!"
Lulu calls, dashing ahead.

The line for the elevators is long, so Lulu and her grandpa take the stairs.
There are a lot of steps, but not too many for Ladybug Girl!

When they get to the dinosaur wing, Lulu cannot believe how giant the titanosaur is.
It's so big that its head and neck poke into a whole other room!

There are a lot of different kinds of dinosaurs,

and their names are about as long as the **entire alphabet.**

"This one is a **stegosaurus,**" Grandpa says.

But just then, Lulu notices *another* dinosaur behind her.

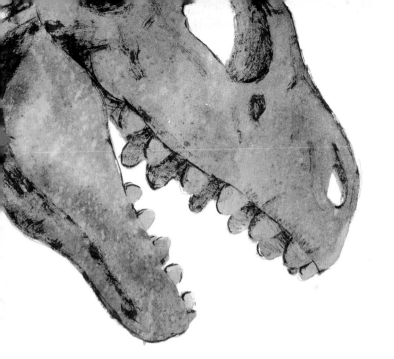

The **tyrannosaurus rex** looks like it is roaring, and Lulu roars right back—

Roar!

ROAR!

ROOOOOOOOAAAAAAR!!!

Grandpa suggests they move on to the Mineral Hall. Gems are much quieter.

Lulu is dazzled by the sparkling minerals
and crystals that line the walls.

"I'll be a queen, Grandpa, and these are all my jewels!"

Then Grandpa shows her something that just about fills the entire room.

"It's a meteorite," he says. "It fell from outer space to earth a long time ago."

Outer space! Lulu realizes there's even more to learn about than she had thought.

And then she remembers:

"We still haven't seen the blue whale!
Come on, Grandpa!"

The blue whale is HUGE.

It floats high above the whole hall.

Lulu feels like they are underwater.

She ice-skates with a walrus

and swims with a sea turtle,

and then she sees a stingray . . .

She'd almost forgotten that she
wanted to learn about stingrays!

How is she going to learn about *everything* in just one day?

"This is what Bingo must feel like
  in the forest when he wants to smell
everything at once." She sighs.

"Lulu bug," Grandpa says,
  "Bingo explores one thing at a time, so he can
fully appreciate it. If you take your time and
  are still for a moment, you'll learn more.

"And there *is* one more place for us to visit," Grandpa adds.

Lulu perks up. "What is it?"

Grandpa leads her through the museum and to a

special door. It opens into a room . . .

. . . that takes Lulu's breath away.

Butterflies of every color flutter around tropical flowers.

The air is warm, and smells like perfume.

Lulu flits around, trying to see a butterfly up close.

But every time she runs near, they fly away.

Grandpa calls her over to see a chrysalis. "It may not look like much, but there are big changes happening to the caterpillar inside."

"Really?" Lulu asks, taking a closer look.
Together they learn about how a caterpillar becomes a butterfly. "It takes some time," her grandpa tells her.
"It doesn't happen overnight."

Then Lulu notices a **big, beautiful yellow butterfly.** She slowly moves closer to it. She stays as still as a flower. Now Lulu can see the cool pattern and **shimmery** texture of its wings, and she can even see its tiny eyes and **antennae!**

She is amazed when it lifts off . . .

and comes to rest on her.

"Hello butterfly!" she whispers.

"I can fly too . . . I am Ladybug Girl!"

After they go to the gift shop, Lulu and Grandpa sit on the museum steps.

"That was really fun!" Ladybug Girl says.

"Even though I didn't learn everything.

Do you know everything now, Grandpa?" she asks him.

"No!" He laughs. "Not even close! You learn new things your entire life.

And since we have more to learn, we'll have to come back to the museum again."

"Yes," agrees Ladybug Girl.

"And then we can spend more time with the bears!"